Mal Peet

Elspeth Graham

Mysterious Traveller

illustrated by

P. J. Lynch

WALKER BOOKS
AND SUBSIDIARIES

LONDON • BOSTON • SYDNEY • AUCKLAND

There were five riders but six camels, travelling fast. Desperately fast. They were being chased, hunted. But because of the fading light and the dust thrown up by the camels' feet they could not tell how close their pursuers were.

The camel without a rider was called Jin-Jin. He was fierce and quick-tempered and very intelligent, which was why he carried the travellers' most precious item of baggage. It was hidden in a woven basket, and Jin-Jin carried it as carefully as he could.

The riders were slithering down into a low and rocky valley when Jin-Jin sensed a new danger. A danger far greater than the men following them. His clever nostrils read it in the air, and he roared a warning, digging his huge feet into the ground.

The rider leading him turned in his saddle and swore angrily. "On, Jin-Jin! On! *On!*" Then his face changed because he saw what Jin-Jin had read on the wind. Behind them, the evening sky was now a boiling wall of sand and dust like a tidal wave.

A desert storm.

There was no time to find shelter. The storm hurtled into the valley and struck the travellers like an enormous fist, blinding them. The howling, whirling brown air blotted out the sun and the rocks and everything except itself.

The riders and their camels vanished into it.

❧   ❧   ❧

Issa, as usual, left his house before dawn and went to watch the sun being born again. At first it was a tiny red glimpse, as if someone had lit a fire among the distant hills. Slowly at first, then more quickly, it grew and swelled until it floated above the hills like a fat, shivery bubble. The colours of the desert came alive.

Issa's old eyes had watched thousands of dawns, but still it seemed to him that each one was a miracle. Each time, it lifted his heart. On this particular morning, however, the bottom edge of the sun was not as bright as usual. Blurry. Veiled. Issa squinted at it, then took a deep breath of the cold desert wind, testing its smell with his nose.

"Mmm," he murmured to himself. "Yes. Something has changed. There has been a storm in the hills, I think."

He turned to go back to his house. It was time for his prayers.

Then he stopped. A flash of bright colour had tickled his eye. A scrap of cloth fluttering from the thorn fence of his goat-pen. He plucked it free and studied it. A ribbon of some sort, richly embroidered in black and green and red, with two golden threads running through it. Issa knew it had not been made by one of his own people. The pattern told him this. This ribbon had travelled a long way. And it was not the kind of thing that anyone would lose or throw away. Issa gazed at the hills for a long moment, thinking. Then he hurried to his house. He said his prayers. He filled a goatskin flask with water and wrapped a flatbread in a cloth. Then he fetched his donkey from her stable.

"Are you in a good mood today, Donkey? Yes? Good, because we have work to do."

The old man climbed onto her back and together they headed out towards the sun.

Issa was a guide. No, not *a* guide. *The* guide. He knew the desert better than any other human being. He knew its tracks and its tricks. He knew its moods and its mountains. In daylight, he could read its colours, its breezes, its shadows. His eyes saw signs where other eyes saw only blank emptiness. At night he could read the map of the stars and the scents threaded on the air. And perhaps because he loved the desert he was never lost in it.

When someone died, people would say, "He has gone where even Issa cannot find him."

Because of his knowledge, because he had magic in his eyes, Issa was an important man. Travellers sought him out. They paid him handsomely to lead them safely through the shifting desert's dangers. And there were many travellers through Issa's small town, most of them traders. They came from the north, their caravans – long lines of camels and donkeys – laden with salt. They came from the south, their caravans laden with gold. The dusty roads they all travelled met in Issa's town.

The traders would ask, "Who can guide us through the maze of hills to the east?" Or, "Who knows where there is water between here and the Great Oasis?"

"Issa," people would say. "You need Issa. His house is that way. Look for the crooked gate."

But on the day that changed his life, Issa and his donkey were alone beneath the hot gaze of the sun.

"Stop, Donkey," Issa said, tapping the animal's neck. "Let us stop and think."

They had been travelling for several hours and had come to the low wall of the hills. The ways in had been hidden by the storm. Issa stared, working out how the world had become different. Then the donkey's ears twitched.

"What?" Issa said.

The donkey's ears twitched again, and this time Issa heard something that sounded like a human cough, or groan.

"Good girl," he said. "Come on. Take me there."

They struggled into a shallow valley. Issa had been here before; but its shape had been changed by disaster.

The donkey stopped again. Another harsh cry, louder and closer now. Where the grey rock wall of the valley rose out of the sand, something moved. Squinting, Issa made out the neck and head, the shoulders and hump of a camel. The rest of its body was buried in sand, pressed against the rock. It roared when Issa approached, and showed its big yellowish teeth.

"Salaam," Issa said quietly. "Peace, Camel. I mean you no harm."

The animal studied the old man suspiciously. Issa stood, keeping his distance. He was puzzled. Clearly the camel was kneeling. He should have been strong enough to get to his feet, to lift himself free of the sand and dust, but he had chosen not to. Why?

Then a cry, a tiny cry, leaked into the hot air. The camel turned his head and flared his nostrils.

Issa now saw that behind the animal there was a split in the wall of stone, like a very narrow cave. He moved forward, slowly and cautiously, murmuring soft words. "Easy, Camel sir, easy. Here, smell my hand. I would prefer it if you did not bite it. Good. Thank you."

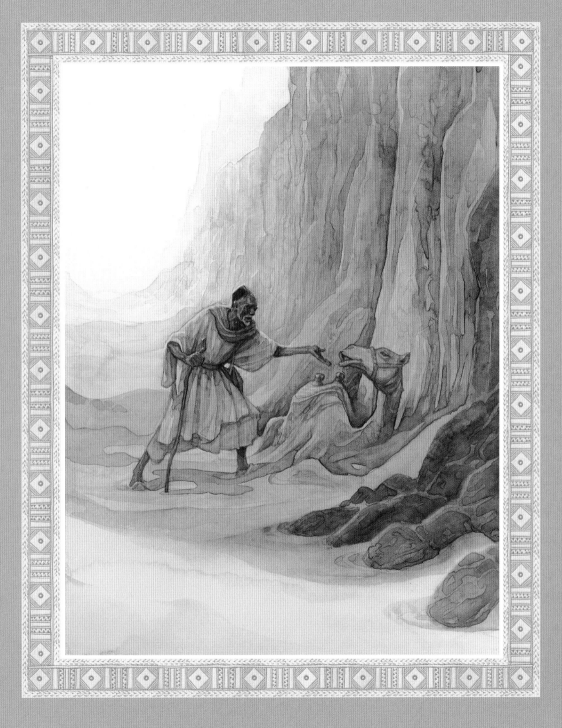

Now Issa was close enough to see that the camel's bridle was embroidered in the same red, black and green pattern as the ribbon he had found at sunrise. Except that woven into the bridle were letters. A word.

"Jin-Jin? Is that your name? Jin-Jin?"

The camel's ears swivelled forwards. Yes.

"Jin-Jin. Well, Jin-Jin, you must trust me. Please stand up, my friend. Up."

Another thin cry came from within the rock. A human cry.

The camel hesitated, then began to move. Heaving himself free of the sand, unfolding his long legs. Standing. Yet he did not seem to want to leave the wall of rock.

Issa took hold of his bridle and made encouraging noises. "Chuh-chuh-cher. Come, Jin-Jin. Chuh-chuh."

And at last Jin-Jin trusted Issa enough to move. He stepped out into the hot gaze of the sun.

"Good," Issa said, patting the camel's shoulder. "Now let us see what you were so anxious to protect from the storm."

Issa opened the woven basket and his heart stumbled. A child's eyes were looking up at his.

Once, many years earlier, a trader had shown Issa a black

pearl. It had a gleam deep inside it. This child, this baby, had huge black pearls for eyes. Her body was wrapped in finest, softest cotton. Something made of gold hung from a cord around her neck, something the shape of half a star. There were letters hammered into the gold, but Issa could not make sense of them.

The child scrunched her eyes shut and wailed.

Issa stepped back and looked up at the sky. "Why," he asked it, "did you send such a gift to an old man?"

Issa named the child Mariama and brought her up. The townspeople decided that she was his grandchild and he did not deny it. He took her everywhere with him. Before she learned to walk she was familiar with the donkey's jerky trot and Jin-Jin's steady lurch. The travellers and traders who paid

Issa to guide them were puzzled that he had a girl-child with him. Sometimes they teased him.

And Issa would say, "Mariama is a child of the desert. She comes with us to pay her respects to her family. To her uncles, the rocks and hills. To her aunts, the stars. To her four cousins, the winds. How could I leave her at home, when this is her home?"

Perhaps Issa believed this. Or half-believed it. The truth, though, was that love had made them inseparable.

As the years went by, Mariama learned everything that Issa knew: the maps made by the stars, the shimmering paths through the hills, the weather foretold by dawns and sunsets, the messages on the wind, the stories told by stones.

She learned that for a guide everything had a meaning. The shape of a thorn tree, the way sand swirled from the crest of a dune, the length and colour of a shadow, the call of a bird, the height of a cloud.

One evening, Issa was reading aloud from the Qur'an.

He paused in his reading and said, "Please light the lamps, Mariama."

She looked up, puzzled. "The lamps are already lit, Grandfather."

He lifted his head. "Ah, yes," he said. "So they are."

A few mornings later, she watched his hand searching for the bowl of coffee she'd put in front of him. She watched him fumbling to open the gate to the goat-pen.

And she understood. Her blood turned as cold as the water from the well.

She waited for him to tell her, and at last he did. "I am going blind, my child," he said simply. "My old eyes are dying faster than the rest of me."

All Mariama could say was, "Yes, Grandfather. I know."

❧　❧　❧

Darkness descended quickly on Issa. Within a few weeks he was using a stick to feel his way between the house and the stable. One morning Mariama found him standing by the fence with his face lifted towards the rising sun.

He said, "Is it beautiful, child?"

"Yes, Baba."

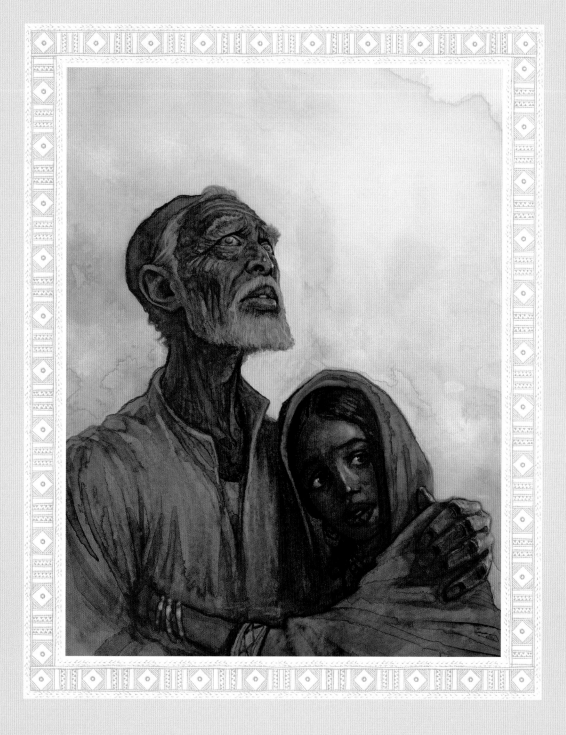

Issa nodded. "Yes. I have a thousand memories of it, thanks be to God, which is enough. But I have been thinking, Who will pay a guide who is blind? How will we live?"

Mariama had no answer, so she put her arm around her grandfather's waist. He put his hand on her small shoulder.

After a silence he said, "I found a baby in the desert. It was a sort of miracle. But my first thought was that it was unfair for an old man to be burdened with a child; that trouble had been sent into my life. I was wrong, of course. God has plans that we understand only afterwards, in darkness. You were a gift. I thought the gift was love, but it was even more than that."

Mariama understood. "Yes, Baba. I was sent to be your eyes."

So now Mariama had another skill to learn: how to use words to show Issa the things that his eyes could not see.

"We are below the rock shaped like a lizard," she would say. Or, "The cloud is like the skin of a grey fish." Or, "Now we are passing the line of thorn trees that look like old women lifting their shawls over their heads."

"Yes," Issa might say. "Good, Mariama. That is what they are like. I always thought so."

And in this way, with his long memory and Mariama as his eyes, Issa was still the greatest of all guides. When travellers asked for help, the townspeople said, "You need Issa and his granddaughter. They live that way – the house with the crooked gate."

Then, late one afternoon, three strangers came to the house. One was taller than a door and fierce-looking, with a scar on his face that began beside his left eye and disappeared into his beard. Two other men stood behind him. One was old with a nose like a hawk's beak. The other was young. His dark eyes were restless, as if keen to remember everything they saw. When Mariama asked them to come inside, Scarface and Hawknose stood aside to allow the young man to enter first.

Ah, Mariama thought. So he is the important one.

While she boiled water for tea she studied him, secretly. And if Issa had been able to see, he might have recognized the pattern in the embroidery that trimmed his robes.

Issa and the visitors made a little polite conversation while evening shadows filled the room.

Then Scarface cleared his throat and got down to business. "We are heading for Ahara," he said.

Issa nodded. "A tiresome journey, but not a difficult one. The salt caravans go there all the time. Team up with one of them. You will not get lost."

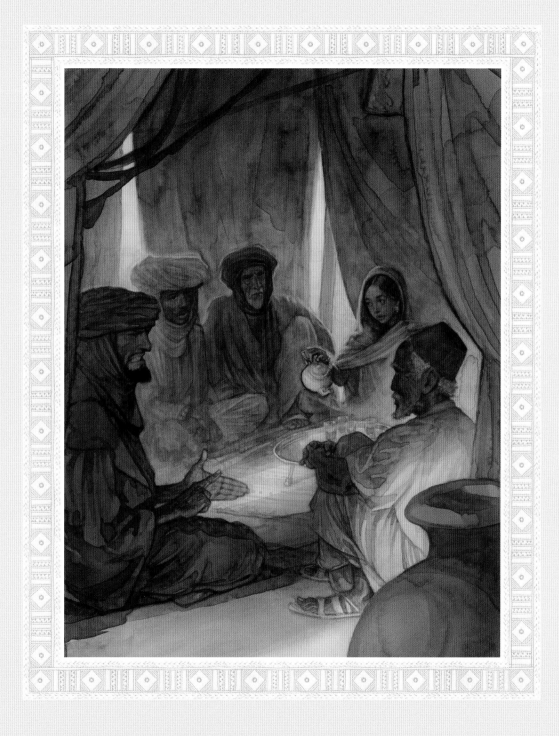

"We do not have time for that," Scarface said. "The caravans go round the Bitter Mountains. We want to go *through* them, which will save us at least six days' travelling. We are in a hurry. And we are told that only you know the way."

"Perhaps," Issa said. "But it is harsh and dangerous, and there is no water in the mountains. Besides, I am an old man, as you see. I do not think I have the strength for such a journey." He sighed and shook his head. "Forgive me, but I cannot help you."

Mariama saw Scarface turn to look at the young man, who made a little gesture with his head. A gesture that gave permission.

Scarface reached inside his robe and produced something that he dropped into Issa's lap. "Perhaps this will change your mind," he said.

Mariama watched her grandfather's old but clever fingers untie the little bag and feel what was inside it.

Pearls. Issa's fingers counted them. There were a great many. He felt their perfect shape and glossiness. They were like an angel's tears fallen to earth. Priceless.

Recently, when he should have been sleeping, Issa had been worrying about Mariama. What would become of her when

he died? How would she live? Who would marry an orphaned girl with no money? Now these questions came into his head once more. And it seemed to him that the heavy little bag in his hand contained the answers. He sighed again. "Wealth does not always bring happiness," he said finally. "But poverty always brings sorrow. Your offer is too generous to refuse, kind sirs. I will guide you through the Bitter Mountains."

"Thank you," Scarface said. "Excellent."

The visitors finished their tea and got to their feet.

Scarface said, "So, we will meet tomorrow, God willing."

"Yes," Issa said. "At sunrise, God willing. Mariama, fetch me my stick."

She brought it and put it into his hand and helped him to stand. He used the stick to find his way to the door. An awful silence filled the room.

Hawknose ended it. "Old man, can you not see? Are you blind?"

"Yes," Issa said, surprised. "Did you not know? Were you not told?"

Another silence.

Hawknose narrowed his eyes. "A blind guide? Is this some sort of joke? Some sort of trick?"

Mariama felt hot blood rise to her face. She stepped forward and spoke. "Sirs, no one has deceived you. My grandfather knows this land like no other. As if it were his own hand. I am his eyes. You can trust us. Ask anyone."

"Pah!" Scarface said, scowling, and tore the pouch of pearls from Issa's hand. "Let us go, master. These people think we are fools."

The young man said nothing. He looked into Mariama's eyes for the first time. There was a question in his face but he did not ask it. Then he turned away and led his companions out of the house.

❧   ❧   ❧

Early the following morning, Mariama went to fetch water from the well.

When she returned Issa said, as usual, "What news, child?"

The village well was the place for gossip. When she went for water, she was her grandfather's ears, too.

Mariama filled the kettle. "They have left," she said. "The young man and the other two. Soon after dawn. Heading for the Bitter Mountains."

"What? Without a guide?"

"Yes. The young man has a magic stone shaped like a finger. When he hangs it from a string it always points to the north. He says he would rather follow his magic stone than a guide who cannot see."

Issa grunted and stroked his chin. "Birds have the same magic stone in their heads," he said eventually. "That is how they find their way. But birds can fly over mountains and over seas. Men cannot." The old man took his stick and tapped his way out into the yard.

Mariama followed him. He lifted his face to the sky. He licked his finger and held it up to measure the wind. Mariama waited.

"Saddle Jin-Jin," Issa said at last. "And prepare us for a journey. Make haste, child."

The sun had already begun its climb down the sky when Mariama brought Jin-Jin to a halt. Her sharp eyes studied the sandy, stony ground. "They left the caravan route here, Baba. They turned north, towards the mountains."

Issa tutted his tongue against his teeth. "Can you read their tracks?"

"Yes, I think so."

"Good. We'll follow."

Late in the afternoon they stopped again. The twisting trail had taken them, slowly, higher and higher. Now the ground beneath the camel's feet was hard rock.

Mariama could no longer see the travellers' tracks. "I have lost them, Grandfather," she confessed.

"Hmm. Perhaps," Issa said. "Tell me where we are. Tell me what you see."

A valley lay ahead of them. Its walls were of great brown rock piled up like books that might belong to a giant. In their shadows, big-bellied baobab trees lifted their thick branches and fingery leaves into the air like a line of fat old ladies dancing. In the distance beyond the valley, huge towers of rock rose into the air, carved into fantastic shapes by the

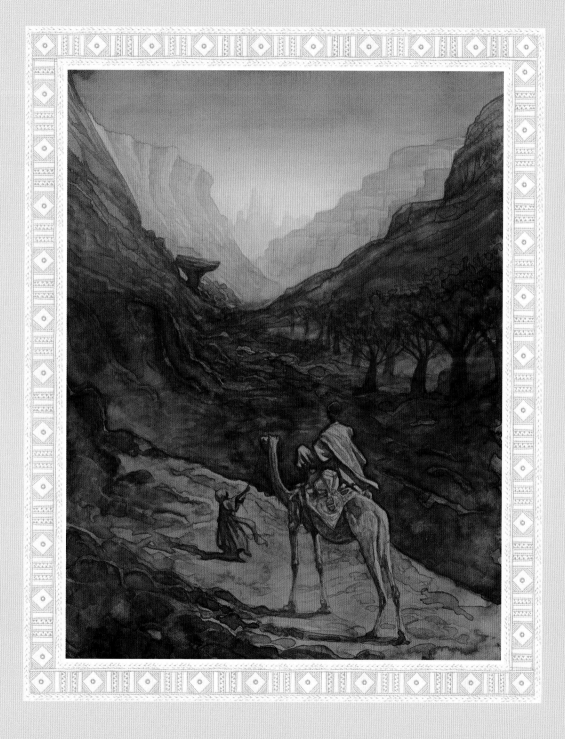

desert winds. In the late sun they looked as though they had been cut from purple paper and glued to the sky.

Mariama described all this to her grandfather.

He nodded approvingly, then asked, "How much of the day is left?"

The western sky was turning the colour of a sea-coral bracelet.

"Only an hour," Mariama said.

The old man grunted. "So," he said. "Look down into the valley. Can you see a big rock the shape of a boat, balanced on another rock? Looking as if it should fall?"

"Yes, Grandfather. I see it."

"Good. We will camp there for the night."

In the morning, her grandfather shook Mariama awake. The stars were fading into the dawn. She blew life back into the fire and she and Issa sat close to it wrapped in their blankets.

After a while, Issa said, "Is it light enough to see yet?"

"Yes, Grandfather, just."

He pointed with his stick. "Can you see a little path over there, going up? Yes? Follow it to the top of the cliff, then come back and tell me what you saw. And be careful, child."

Mariama climbed the steep path. It was just a crack in the rock. In places it was only a little wider than her body. When at last she reached the top, she stood wide-eyed and hardly able to breathe.

The mountains stretched before her to the very edge of distance. Some had peaks that were flat-topped and grooved like huge and ancient teeth. Others were bent and twisted like goats' horns, while others were slender and pointed like minarets. And they were all a deep, dark blue, like the scarves of the camel-traders who came from the north. But then, as Mariama watched, the light of the rising sun touched the tips of the mountains and painted them a glowing, burning gold.

She cried out aloud because she had never seen anything so beautiful, so magical. And as the sun climbed higher, the golden light slid down the teeth, the horns, the minarets. The blue drained away, and now she saw that dark valleys curled among the mountains like the roots of a tree. And from one of these valleys, not far away, arose a little twist of smoke.

She turned and hurried down the cliff path.

Issa was standing waiting for her. "What did you see?"

"I cannot describe it, Baba. I do not have the words."

Her grandfather smiled. "No. I have stood where you stood, trying to think in words. But tell me, did you see smoke?"

"Yes."

"In which direction? How far away?"

Mariama told him.

"Yes," Issa said, "that would be the strangers' fire. These valleys are a maze, and already they are lost. Now, let us make coffee."

"But Grandfather, should we not set off after the travellers, if they are lost?"

"No. That valley is a dead end. They will have to come back the way they came. Then we will go to meet them. We have time for breakfast."

Issa was wrong. Perhaps, if his eyes had been good, he would have seen that the sun had a cloudy grey belly when it rose above the mountains.

They had been riding for an hour
when he said, "Hss, Jin-Jin. Stop."

Mariama looked at him.
"What is it, Baba?"

Issa did not answer. The silence that surrounded them was as thick as a fleece. No birds called from the thorn trees. No insects hissed or chirruped from the rocks.

"Grandfather?"

"The wind is wrong," Issa said, as if talking to himself. "What colour is the sky?"

Looking up, Mariama saw that it was as white as paper. A flock of desert sparrows flew across it, panicking.

Jin-Jin tossed his head and groaned. Suddenly Mariama was afraid.

"On," Issa said. "Hurry."

They climbed out of one valley and rode down into the next. In the distance, three shapes wobbled in the heat-haze.

"There!" Mariama cried. "I can see them, Baba! They are coming back this way, just as you said they would."

Mariama urged Jin-Jin onwards to meet the travellers, but he resisted. He groaned deep in his throat and tried to turn back.

And then Mariama saw why.

The lower edge of the sky had changed again; now it was yellowy-purple, the colour of an old bruise. A hot and sudden gust of wind, full of grit, hit Mariama in the face. The riders had felt it too. They looked over their shoulders, then whipped their camels into a gallop. A boiling brown cloud loomed over the valley.

"A sandstorm, Grandfather!" Mariama cried. "A sandstorm, coming at us!"

"I feared so," Issa said grimly. "Now listen to me, child. Look over to our right. Can you see a split in the cliff, like a tall shadow?"

"I can see many, Grandfather."

"Look again. Can you see one that is darker than the others? One bent like a dog's leg?" His voice was calm and steady.

The riders were close now, but the storm was swarming into the valley behind them like a pack of hungry wolves.

Mariama swallowed her fear and studied the face of the cliff. "Yes," she said. "I see it."

"Good," her grandfather said. "That is our place of safety. Take us there, Mariama. And make this stubborn camel run like the wind!"

"This way!" Mariama yelled, pointing. "Follow us!"

The three travellers hesitated, their eyes wide with fear; but when Mariama turned Jin-Jin and charged towards the cliff, they followed. Sand lifted from the ground in stinging whirlwinds. The sky darkened and moaned.

When they reached the cliff, Mariama's heart sank. The gap in the rock seemed hardly big enough to shelter one camel, let alone four. She turned to Issa, the flying sand biting her face. "We have come to the wrong place, Baba! There is nothing here!"

Issa slid from Jin-Jin's back onto the ground. "Trust me, child," he said, and felt for the camel's reins. "And you, Jin-Jin, sir, must trust me too."

The split in the rock was narrow, but deeper than Mariama had thought. Issa led them into it, feeling his way with his hand. The harsh stone scraped Jin-Jin's flanks. He groaned and lowered his head but went on. Mariama was afraid; she felt as though the huge cliff was closing in on her, crushing her.

Then, suddenly, they were in a great space. A cave! Thin beams of light from the opening lit up its sandy floor, but its walls and roof were lost in darkness.

One by one the three travellers followed them in, soothing

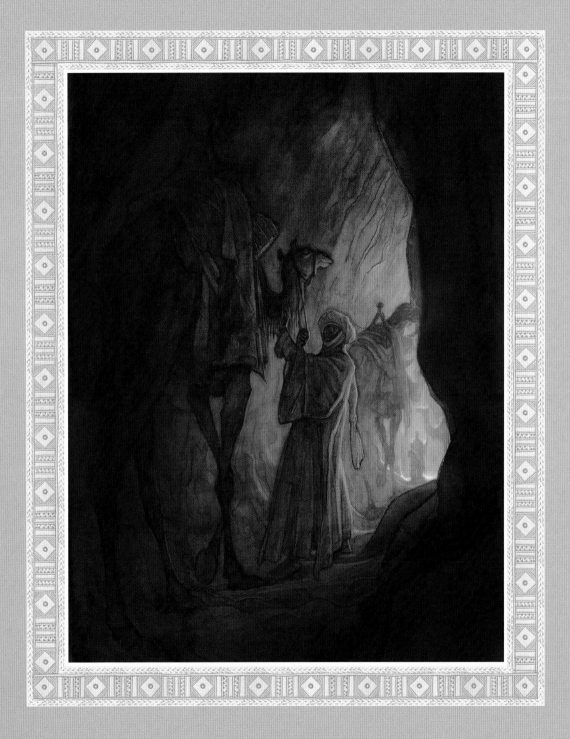

their nervous camels as they entered the cool darkness. Scarface was the last. He looked about him and began to say something, but his words were lost in a great wave of sound. The desert storm roared past the cave and filled it with deafening noise. The last beams of sunlight went out like snuffed candles.

A long hour passed. Then at last the storm, with a last whip of its tail, vanished into the distance. Silently, daylight spread its fingers into the cave.

The young man was the first to speak. "Thanks be to God."

"Indeed," Issa said. "Now Mariama will lead us home. Then, when you and your animals are rested, you can set off again for Ahara. And this time, I think, you will take the safe route around the mountains, yes?"

*   *   *

Two mornings later, the young traveller came again to Issa's house. This time he was alone. When Mariama let him in, he bowed to her and smiled. Blushing, she put the kettle on the stove to make coffee, then sat in her corner of the room.

The young man had come, he said, to show his gratitude

and to beg Issa's forgiveness. He apologized for his men's mocking of Issa's blindness, for their insults. He praised Issa's knowledge of the desert. He congratulated Issa on the bravery and intelligence of his granddaughter, which made Mariama blush again.

"My comrades and I are about to leave," he said. "I came to say farewell and to give you this." He lifted Issa's hand and put the pouch of pearls into it.

The old man felt it with his fingers, then handed it back. "I cannot accept this," he said. "I did not guide you to Ahara."

"No. You did much more than that. You saved our lives."

"Yes, praise God," Issa said. "But not for payment."

The young man frowned, uncertain what to do. Then he went to Mariama and put the pouch on the floor close to her. He held his finger to his lips, bidding her to say nothing. Then he froze, staring down at her. "Where did you get that?" he demanded. "The gold pendant you wear around your neck?"

His voice was suddenly stern, and Mariama was alarmed. Her hand flew to the pendant as if to protect it.

"Tell me," the young man insisted.

"I have always had it, sir. I was wearing it when … when Grandfather found me."

"Found you? What do you mean, 'found you'?"

Mariama bit her lip. There were things that only she and Baba knew. Was she now to share them with this stranger?

Issa came to her rescue. He said quietly, "I think the pendant has a special meaning for you. Am I right, sir?"

"Yes," the traveller said. His eyes remained fixed on Mariama.

Issa nodded. "Please sit," he said, "and I will tell you a story. Or perhaps half a story. It is possible that you know the other half."

So the young man sat beside Mariama while the old man told him how, after a great storm, he had found a bad-tempered camel protecting a baby. That he had brought the child to his house and brought her up. He had always known that the gold pendant marked her out as someone special, that she was a gift that might one day be taken from him.

Then he said, "Are you the one who has come to take her from me?"

Mariama sat folded in a kind of terror. The familiar room suddenly felt strange to her.

Instead of answering Issa's question, the young traveller said, "My name is Abbas. My father is the king of Sana, which borders the Eastern Sea. When I was a boy, ten thousand warriors attacked my father's kingdom. Thinking that he would lose this war, my father sent me north to my uncle's house, where I would be safe. He sent my sister, who was then just a baby, to our other uncle, who lived at the edge of the Great Desert. After many battles, my father and his armies beat the attackers off and saved the kingdom. He sent word for his children to be returned. I was brought home, but my sister could not be found. She had never reached our uncle's house. She and the warriors protecting her had vanished somewhere on their journey. My father could not bring himself to believe that she was dead. We have been looking for her ever since."

Issa had listened intently to Abbas's words. He nodded his head slowly, then spoke. "And how would you know her, if you found her?"

Abbas reached inside his robe and pulled free a gold pendant that hung from his neck by a leather cord. He lifted the cord over his head and held the pendant in his left hand. "She will be wearing the other half of this." He reached his right hand out to Mariama. "Please," he said gently.

She removed her own pendant and gave it to him.

Abbas put the two together. Now they formed a perfect eight-pointed star, and the hammered letters formed the words *Children of Sana, Children of God*.

Mariama stared, wide-eyed. Understanding filled her, like a sunrise.

Abbas said, "Hello, my sister. It has been a long time. Today we have mended our father's heart." And he put his arms around her and held her close.

Tearful rejoicing filled the small room.

"We will leave tomorrow," Abbas said, with laughter in his voice. "I cannot wait to see our father's face. There will be a great feast!"

Mariama's smile clouded over. "Leave? But … I can't. Grandfather needs me. I can't leave him here alone."

"Nonsense," Issa said gruffly. "I shall manage perfectly well."

"No, Baba. I won't go."

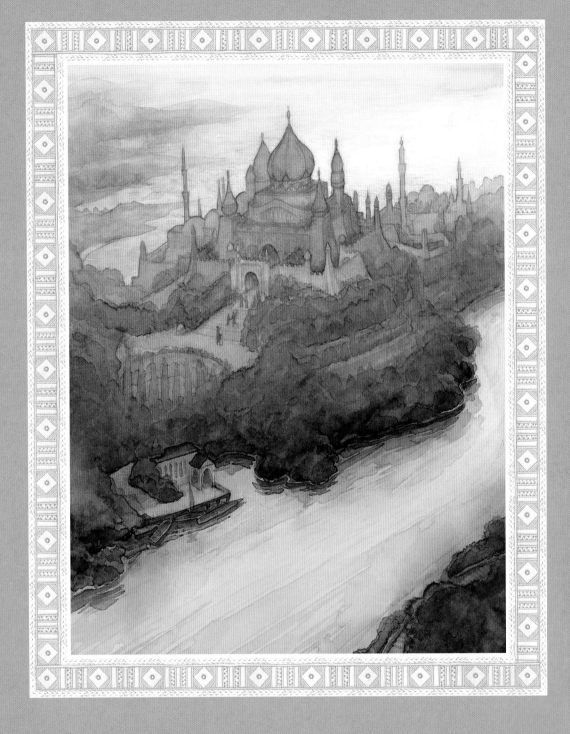

Abbas put his hands on Mariama's shoulders. "Of course you cannot leave your grandfather," he said. He went to the old man and knelt. "Sir," he said. "You must come with us. Stay with us as our honoured guest for as long as you wish. No, please don't argue. My father's palace is a beautiful place, with the great green river on one side and the silver sea on the other. Its courtyards are cool, shaded by trees that blossom all the year round, their flowers white and yellow and blue. There are fountains that throw fans of glittering water into the air. All this will be yours to enjoy."

Issa smiled. "It does indeed sound beautiful," he said, "but you seem to forget. I would not be able to see it."

"Yes you will, Grandfather," Mariama said. "You will see it through my eyes."

And that is exactly what happened.

Authors' Note

This story is set in an imaginary place, but it came about because Elspeth became fascinated by that fabulous and faraway place called Timbuktu. It's in an African country now called Mali, and it's where, long ago, traders bringing salt from the north met traders bringing gold from the south. We began to read and think about those traders, those travellers with their camel caravans, making those long, difficult journeys through mountains and deserts. Their lives, and their livelihoods, depended upon the guides who led them through these dangerous places. When we discovered that one of the most famous of these guides was blind, it set our imaginations racing.